UNEXPECTED

A HOLIDAY SHORT

DL WHITE

Dedication

To my family, blood and chosen:
Thank you for your unending love, support and encouragement
toward achieving my dreams.
To everyone out there wishing for a chance at love. May you find it
and never let go.

The greatest act of
courage is not falling
in love But, despite
everything, falling in
love again.

Robin Wayne Bailey

1

"I DON'T KNOW why you're being so difficult, Saidah. Put on some clothes, run a brush through your hair and come over."

"Maybe I don't want to go over there. Maybe I want to sit on my couch and watch *A Christmas Story* back to back while I drink myself into oblivion." As if I needed to prove my point, I loudly sipped from my mug of spiked hot chocolate.

"That's the exact reason you need to bring your behind over here. You don't need to be by yourself on Christmas. Especially on Christmas."

I rolled my eyes while switching the phone from one shoulder to the other. I was comfortable, deeply implanted into the corner of my new leather couch, under a chenille throw, in my pajamas and fuzzy Christmas socks. The socks weren't necessary, since it was the warmest Christmas Atlanta had seen in years, but they were red and had little green Christmas trees on them, so they were helping to ring in the holiday season as best they could.

The trees on my socks were about the only sign of cheer in my condo. It had been years since I put up a tree and decorated for the season. It had also been years since I joined Faith, my friend-as-close-as-a-sister, and her family for Christmas dinner. My new tradition wasn't one I picked up by choice; it was a natural consequence. And I was in no hurry to change something like a natural consequence.

"I promise you, honey. I'm fine right here. Enjoy your meal and your family. Are we doing after Christmas sales on Saturday?"

Faith sighed that long, drawn out sigh that usually accompanied a roll of her dark brown eyes and pursing of her pouty lips. "Why do you have to ruin everything, you stubborn brat?"

"Wait, what? I didn't know we were name calling on today of all days, the celebration of the birth of sweet little eight pound, six-ounce baby Jesus."

"Yes, we're name calling when you're being stubborn. I was trying to surprise you. Jay is coming to dinner."

My heart skipped a beat at the mention of him. I didn't have to ask for a last name or a clarification on who *Jay* was. I knew very well, and Faith knew, too. The very thought of him brought his face to my memory—strong square jaw with the dimple in the chin, skin like whipped mousse, chiseled cheekbones, classic nose, wide-set eyes so dark they looked black and the longest, prettiest eyelashes you ever saw on a man. Impeccably dressed and intelligent to boot.

Jay was the one that got away.

"Don't lie to me, Faith. Jay is coming to dinner?"

"I wouldn't lie to you, Saidah. Never have, never will."

"Well. When did that happen? How did you even get in touch with him?"

"I have my ways," said Faith. In the background, I heard the clank of the heavy lid to her Le Creuset Dutch oven. A Le Cordon Bleu trained chef that owned a successful catering company, Faith could tear up a meal like nobody's business. You'd swear you were dining at a five-star restaurant and be right in her dining room.

"I'm serious, Faith! How did you manage that? How do you know he's really showing up?"

"Anthony ran into him in Nashville a few weeks ago at that conference he went to — you remember they're in the same frat? They started talking, catching up. He works in... building design or something. Was doing pretty well, but he hinted that his wife left last year."

"Left him? Women are giving up rich, handsome men these days?"

"Girl, I guess. There was an affair, or at least that's the vibe Anthony got from talking to him. Anyway, he seemed to have a hard time, said something about being alone this year, so Anthony invited him over. He came home and told me, and that's when I called you and asked if you were coming over."

As stubborn as I was about spending the day in my pajamas, alone, on my leather couch, the thought of seeing Jay after all these years could be a game changer.

We'd all gone to college together at Albany State University. Jay and Anthony were line brothers in Alpha Psi Alpha. Anthony and Faith were dating and were trying to hook me up with Jay. He and I were friends, then close friends, and then one night after a party, on the walk back to the dorms, he pulled me into the shadow of a building and pressed himself against me, walking me backward until I was caught between the cold brick wall and the warm man with the racing heartbeat.

His lips pressed against mine, tentatively at first and then with a moan and a tilt of his head, deepened the kiss with an open mouth and a probe of his tongue. After a few minutes of breathless kisses and roaming hands, I pulled him from the darkness and around the corner to the side door into the building.

I dragged him to the room that Faith and I shared, that I was pretty much living in alone since she spent a lot of her time at Anthony's place. Jay wasn't my first, but he may as well have been.

Being with him felt so different than the few guys that had stumbled through quick, awkward sex. Jay moved slowly, fluidly, I felt like we were meant to be together. There was definitely no stumbling and zero awkwardness.

After, we talked and talked, tangled up in the sheets with my cheek plastered to his warm skin. I listened to his heartbeat and splayed my fingers across his broad chest, feeling him catch his breath. I was already falling in love.

We were inseparable, unless we were with Faith and Anthony. We were those cute couples that did everything together and always hung out together. Until we weren't.

Jay was from a small South Georgia town and the college experience seemed overwhelming to him. While he did well in classes, he wasn't used to having so many social options. The allure of being able to date *so many women* was tempting. So much so that, before the end of our sophomore year and right after Anthony and Faith got engaged, Jay broke up with me.

Over the next few weeks I saw him on campus, hands tightly clasped around the waist of one girl and then another. Looking into someone else's eyes with that gaze I used to think was reserved for me, laughing that laugh I thought only I could bring out. It devastated me. I tried everything to get him to realize the mistake he'd made, what he was giving up and leaving behind. Jay was more interested in the next party, the next girl, the next conquest.

Faith and I graduated, and a few months later, I walked down the aisle as her Maid of Honor. Though I hadn't seen him in years, Jay was at the wedding, as handsome as he ever was, with a beautiful cinnamon toned woman on his arm.

Twelve years later, we'd be in the same room. Him so handsome, more mature and all grown up; hurt and vulnerable from the demise of his marriage. And me so... well, me.

"So, is he still fine? And what are you making?" I made a

valiant attempt at sounding nonchalant, but Faith was on to me. I could almost hear the grin in her voice, knowing full well what my moments of silence represented.

"I haven't seen him, so I don't know. But Anthony didn't say he'd let himself go or anything. And I'm not going all out — just a bone-in prime rib, garlic mashed potatoes, gravy, collard greens, macaroni and cheese. Maybe a wedge salad with bacon bits, some yeast rolls. Oh, and a Dulce de leche cake. And I'm thinking about whipping up a pound cake with buttercream frosting."

"Not much? Not going all out? I just gained five pounds listening to that."

"Dinner is at three o'clock. I'll save you a place next to Jay. Bring some wine, a nice cabernet or merlot."

"I already told you — what makes you think I've changed my mind?"

"Because I know you. And I know I can *always* change your mind. See you soon."

A dial tone cut my retort short. I rolled my eyes and tossed the phone onto the couch. I stomped to the bedroom, heading straight for the closet. Dressing for this dinner was going to be of utmost importance. I hadn't seen Jay since he paraded that woman in my face and had the nerve to be smug about it.

"Hmmm..." I hummed, stepping into the closet to survey my options. "I'll want to make a good impression... but not look like an attention whore."

I eyed a pair of skinny jeans, dark rinse. My full figure looked ridiculously good in them, but the way Faith cooked, I would need more room than those would allow. "I need to show off my grown and sexy.... but not look thirsty."

I thumbed through a few more options before I grabbed up a brand new black sweater dress with stylish zipper embellishment across each shoulder. It hugged my ample hips and showed off my bust in glorious fashion. At a perfect mid-thigh length, it was long enough to be classy but short enough to be sexy. I'd pair it with my over-the-knee, three-inch suede boots.

I plugged in my flatiron and turned on the shower. I was going to be a spectacle or die trying.

Time to show Jay what he'd been missing all these years.

2

———

"MERRY CHRISTMAS!" Faith bellowed as soon as she opened the door. She had a toddler perched on one hip and a shy four-year-old behind her legs.

I stepped into the house, my heels clicking on the marble inlay. Anthony did very well as a software consultant and Faith's catering business added to the pot. The Thomas family lived very well, in a near-palatial estate in affluent Alpharetta. You'd never know it by looking at them, though. They were the most down-to-earth people I had ever met, generous to a fault and always happy to lend a helping hand or a word of advice where needed.

"I'm not sure you need this wine. Sounds like you've already had enough to drink." I handed Faith the two bottles of wine I had picked up—I couldn't decide between a cabernet or merlot, so I brought both — and I took the baby from her arms.

"Can't I just be happy to see you? It's been years since you were here on Christmas. Come on in, make yourself at home."

"Wait!" I hissed at Faith before she veered off to the kitchen. "Is... is he here?"

She rolled her eyes. "Did you miss that Range Rover in the driveway? That's not mine, and you know Anthony is a Denali guy." I hadn't missed the ebony black SUV with the shiny alloy wheels hogging most of the driveway.

She set the bottles of wine near a small but growing collection of wines on the counter and reached for Avery, who nearly launched out of my arms into hers. Ashley followed closely behind her mother.

"Hello Miss Ashley, acting like you don't know me." She smiled and ducked out of sight. It always took her a minute to warm up to me. "I see you back there. We'll talk later, okay?"

Faith pushed me toward the living room with her fingertips. "Stop stalling. Go. Make a good impression."

I sucked in a deep breath and stepped down the hall into the formal living room where Anthony was holding court near the stone fireplace, his glass half full of something dark. The tree was the focal point of the room, grandiose and glamorous, impressive in both height and decoration. Faith changed the theme and colors every year. This year the bulbs were deep ruby red satin and glittering gold that reflected the softly glowing pearl lights perfectly. The red velvet tree skirt, unfurled and surrounding the tree so elegantly, was the perfect touch.

"She outdid herself this year," said Anthony, from across the room. "Our biggest tree yet. Had to decorate half of it from upstairs."

"She is a big one," I agreed with a smile. "Merry Christmas, Anthony. Did you guys open the gifts from me?"

He nodded. "The girls love their Misty Copeland Barbies. We set them up right next to the Ava dolls. And I'm digging this G-Shock watch."

He flicked his wrist to show off the watch I'd gotten him. That didn't really go with the casual look he was going for with slacks, a long-sleeved shirt and vest, but I appreciated the sentiment.

"Faith loved the Tiffany pendant you got her. I was a little scared, because I had a blue box under the tree for her too. But I'm sure you ladies will chat about that."

"So... uh..." I glanced around the room to find it empty, save myself, Anthony and another gentleman that looked familiar, but I couldn't place him. "Where is Jay? I wanted to say hello."

"Jay had to step outside to take a phone call. He'll be right back. But this is his brother, Will."

Less than interested in some counterfeit version of Jay but not wanting to seem rude, I stepped forward and shook the hand offered to me. "Nice to meet you," I mumbled with a smile. He replied with something similar. He was handsome and looked just like his brother. He just... wasn't Jay.

The door to the patio swung open and in walked Jay, tucking a mobile phone into the pocket of a pair of dark jeans. He was a taller, broader, even more handsome version of the Jay I used to know. He wore black loafers and a grey cashmere V-neck sweater with a shirt under it, the collar unbuttoned enough to reveal the neck I used to love to plant kisses around.

"Jay. Hello. It's been a long time."

The words tumbled out of my mouth as I walked—no, *glided* across the room toward him. I extended a hand and gave him my warmest smile, which I hoped would let him know that I harbored no hard feelings toward him. I was older, wiser, more mature, a better woman than I had been so many years ago.

"Hey, what's up," he said, brushing past me. I stood there, looking like a fool, my hand still extended for more than a few seconds before spinning on my heels and turning around. I watched Jay pick up a glass and shoot back a mouthful of liquor.

"Was that who I think it was?" Will asked him.

Jay nodded. "Yeah. Yeah, it's all good. We can sign paperwork on Monday."

"Yeah? Congrats on that, bro!" Will's face lit up as he stretched an arm out to his brother. They bumped fists and made irritating grunting sounds at each other. To Anthony, Will said, "Jay here just closed the deal for us to remodel that old beat up strip mall off of Panola Road. The plan is to tear most of it down, reconfigure the interior, redo the facades. It'll be a multi-million dollar deal. Not our biggest project but our most public facing for sure."

"So..." I stepped into the room and tried to wiggle my way into the conversation. "You two run a renovation business? Or something?"

"Yes, that's exactly what we do," answered Will. "Hunter Construction does commercial structure renovation. Like when a company buys an old, previously existing building and wants to retrofit it to a vision for the new place? They call us."

"Sounds interesting. And profitable. You must be the muscle," I purred, sidling up next to Jay, gripping his arm. It was deliciously meaty inside the soft fabric of the sweater. Jay stared at me, those dark eyes locked on mine. Then his gaze slid down until they reached my hand on his arm. He looked up at me again and stepped away, conveniently removing my touch.

"Okay if I refill?" He didn't wait for an answer; instead heading toward the expansive bar on the other side of the tree.

Confused, I shot a glance at Anthony. He shrugged and took a sip of his drink. In the corner, Jay was loudly tossing ice cubes into a glass. Will watched him for a moment, his brows furrowed deeply, before glancing at me with an apologetic smile.

I didn't bother to smile back. I turned around and stomped into the spacious kitchen where I found Faith spooning aujus over the prime rib on a festive red serving platter. In multicolored dishes around the kitchen, attractively prepared sides waited to be whisked to the buffet in the dining room. The entire room smelled delicious.

"How'd it go?" she asked, her brows high upon her forehead. I shook my head and headed toward the wine, snatching a glass from its fancy storage system.

I plucked the bottle of merlot from the collection of wines, pulled a drawer handle, retrieved the opener and went at the bottle, aggressively wrenching and twisting until the cork popped. I wasted no time in filling a bulbous glass.

"Pour me one," she ordered, carting the aromatic roast past me and depositing it on the center of the buffet. When she came back, I had a glass waiting for her, but I was working on gulping mine down.

I was fuming. Absolutely fuming.

Faith angled her head to peek around the corner as she took a sip of wine. "Did you talk to him?"

"Mmmhmm!" I gulped down more wine while I cut my eyes at her, and then toward the living room.

"What's that look for? What happened?"

"I *tried* to speak to that fool. He didn't even say hello. Said, *hey what's up* and walked right past me. Then I tried again; I put my hand on his arm, paid him a nice little compliment. He looked at me like my hands were dripping with acid and moved away from me."

"He did what? Like how?"

I eyed her like Jay had eyed me, then mimicked him stepping away. She mused, sipping her wine.

"Maybe he needs to warm back up to you. Give him a little time. You're sitting next to him at dinner — plenty of time to get reacquainted."

She set down her wineglass and grabbed mine. "Help me carry this stuff to the buffet so we can sit down to eat."

3

———

"So… Jay. What keeps you busy these days?"

Faith refused to move me to a different seat, despite my begging. She was convinced he just needed a hot meal and some time to warm up to me and he would be fine. I wasn't so sure about that.

"Work," he bit out. "I've been building my business for the last ten years." Then he dipped his head and stabbed at a mound of green beans, stuffing them into his mouth.

"Oh. Well, that's good. You're winning contracts, so it looks like all that work has paid off. What about in your off time? Are you still playing—"

"Nah," he said, grumbling, shaking his head. "I don't get into too much outside of gym time."

Surprised, an eyebrow shot up. I always knew him as an outgoing young man, involved in sports and myriad campus clubs. "Really? You used to play on the intramural football league. And you guys always sponsored Game Night. Remember when we'd get a bunch of board games and card games together, some drinks–"

"Ooh, those were fun," Faith said, jumping in. "I was the Scattergories Queen!"

"Yeah, well, some people grow up past their college days," said Jay, swiping the corner of his mouth with a napkin. "Some people have business to take care of and can't be running the streets like they don't have any responsibilities."

"Who's running the streets like they don't have responsibility?" I asked. "Everyone needs an outlet for relaxation and stress release. Maybe you need to pick up a hobby."

Jay paused, then slowly rolled his eyes over to me. I stared him down, daring him to step over the imaginary line in the sand I'd just drawn. "Are you trying to say something to me?"

"You seem uptight, is all I'm saying."

"I don't give a shit what you think—"

"Obviously."

"... so you can keep your opinions–"

"Jay. Saidah." Faith's voice was low but stern, and even though I was a grown woman, I knew she meant business. Then she smiled. But I saw right through that fakery. "It's Christmas. Let's not."

"Tell *her* to let's not. She's the one over here deciding what folks need." His chair scraped roughly against the hardwood floor as he pushed back. "I *need* to refill my drink."

I watched a beet-red pallor cross Anthony's complexion. "Hey, man. Take it easy on my floors. We just got them re-done last spring."

"Nobody cares about your damn floors," he mumbled, shuffling away from the table, headed toward the bar.

I eyed Faith, but she was glaring at her husband, who gave her a helpless shrug of his shoulder and wide-eyed stare.

"Uhm..." Will cleared his throat, eyeing his brother out of the corner of his eye. "The... the prime rib — it's delicious. Everything is just great. I like the macaroni and cheese. I dabble a bit in the kitchen, but this is on another level. Do you use gruyere in your bechamel sauce?"

"Yes," she said, brightening. "I do. You have quite the cultured palate. Thank you, Will." Faith graciously accepted the compliment, a smile on her lips but worry in her eyes as Jay approached the table, his glass brimming with dark liquid. He dropped into his chair and dug into his meal again.

"Yeah. It's all great." He picked up a knife and began sawing at a slice of fork tender beef, scraping against Faith's fine china. "I sure appreciate this pity meal y'all invited me to since my wife left me and moved in with some broke ass–"

"Jay," said Will, his voice at the bottom of his throat, practically growling through clenched teeth. "Take it *easy*, man."

"And the bitch is asking for fucking alimony, like I wanna pay her to *not* be married to me. Fuck her, man. She can marry that broke nigga she left me for. Let him buy her Gucci and Prada, let him pay her credit card bills."

He dropped his knife, sending a spray of Au jus across his chest. "Shit. This is fuckin' cashmere, goddammit. Why y'all got these weak ass knives for cutting meat?"

Faith hopped up from the table and sprang into action. "Take it off. I have some club soda I can treat it with and I'll put it in the steamer. Won't hurt it at all."

Jay's limbs were loose; his words slurred as he pulled the sweater over his head and tossed it at her. She took it and escaped to the laundry room. He resumed his seat in his undershirt and jeans.

I reached for my glass of wine and sipped. I sure was glad I left my calm and peaceful condo to share dinner with a drunken boor. He had the demeanor—and the capacity—of a man that had been drinking for a long time. No wonder his wife had left him. I felt like I'd dodged a bullet, myself.

"Don't care about her anyway," Jay quietly raged, before inserting a forkful of food into his mouth. "Got bitches everywhere that want to be with me. One right next to me that won't leave me alone. Hey Will," he said, his head lobbing toward his brother, across the table. "Why don't you tell her I don't date fat bitches?"

"That's just fine, Will," I responded, giving him a bright smile. "Because I don't date sloppy drunk assholes. Excuse me."

I pushed my chair back from the table, picked up my plate and marched into the kitchen. I ran into Faith on her way from the laundry room.

"Thanks for dinner, honey. I'm out of here."

"Nooo..." Faith's eyes bugged out and reached for me, wrapping her thin fingers around my arms. "Do not leave me alone with these men! Anthony won't say anything and Jay is so damn drunk–"

"That drunk just called me a fat bitch." I grabbed my purse from the alcove next to the refrigerator where I'd left it when I came in. "I don't care how handsome he used to be or how much I thought I loved him. I'm not sitting through one more second of *that*." I jabbed my finger toward the dining room where it sounded like Jay was getting started again.

I leaned toward Faith and dropped a kiss on her cheek. "Merry Christmas. Thanks for the Gucci clutch. Can't wait to break it in. Ya'll try to have a good day."

The sound of my heels echoed up into the high ceiling as I headed toward the front door, pulled it open and started down the sidewalk toward my car. I stopped long enough to gawk at the Range Rover rudely parked diagonally across the driveway. It looked as if Jay had arrived drunk and got worse.

The front door opened, and Will stepped out, rushing down the steps. He and Jay had similar features, but obviously Will was younger. He stopped when he was a few steps from me and shoved his hands into grey-black distressed jeans. His sweater, a rich cranberry, looked nice against his lighter skin tone.

"Uh... I didn't... I'm sorry; I never caught your name."

I glared at him for a moment or two before I answered. "Saidah. Saidah Harland." As if on automatic, I offered him a hand. He took it like he was going to shake it, but he held it in his hands, stroking it between his palms. "Your brother is an asshole and a drunkard. I'm sure you know this, so why you let him jump all over me and didn't say a thing–"

"Ms. Harland... Saidah. Jay's actually my half brother, but they raised together us, so..." He lifted and lowered his shoulders in a shrug. "Anyway. That's why I came out. To apologize for him, for the way he treated you and the things he said. It was uncalled for and I should have stepped in earlier."

"Well..." My hand felt warm, enclosed in his. My body felt warm under the gaze of his espresso brown eyes. "I... thank you. For the apology. I appreciate it."

"You're not taking off, are you? Because of him?"

"I didn't want to come over here anyway, but Faith said he was coming to dinner and I thought maybe..." I shook my head, then looked down at our hands, mine still intertwined in his. "I guess you really can't go home again."

"He..." Will turned to look back at the house, like he could see through the brick exterior to the scene in the dining room. "Jay's had a rough time of it, the last few years. The business hit a rough patch and his wife got impatient with the restructure. She left last year, but as you heard, she's holding out for a ridiculous amount of alimony now that the business is doing well again."

I nodded, understanding. Not forgiving, but it helped to know where the vitriol was coming from. "I appreciate the explanation. He's still pretty loose with his mouth and I *don't* appreciate that."

"I completely understand and I'm sure when he gets right,

he'll be embarrassed at himself. But I was hoping I could make up for my brother's behavior."

I pulled my hand from his, warm as it was, and started inching toward my car. "I don't need you to make up for him. I need him to do better." ·

"Please. Don't... don't go. You haven't even had dessert yet and—"

"Is that another crack about my weight? What is it with you two? A woman is bigger than a toothpick and she's suddenly too fat for you?" I propped my hands on my hips and lifted my chin in defiance.

"No!" He said, almost shouted. "Saidah... no. That wasn't a crack about your weight. And not that you need me to tell you you look amazing, but... you look amazing."

His eyes skipped down my figure and back up, lingering at my chest. I lifted my hands to block his vision and glared. "I'm sorry. My brother may not be interested—actually, I think he's too drunk to be interested in anything, but I really appreciate what you've got goin' on here."

"Hunh," I grunted, eyeing him. "You're not... weird or anything, are you?"

He laughed, showing off a wide smile of straight white teeth. He had a small dimple high on his left cheek. "Uh, no. I'm not weird. I don't think I am, anyway. Faith was telling me about you before you got here. How you work with at-risk kids and volunteer at the nursery at Children's Healthcare. How you two have been friends since your first day at Albany. And how you and Jay were together for a while. He must have lost his damn mind or something, because if he let a woman like you get away he had to have been crazy."

"My sentiments exactly. All this flattery aside, I need to get going. I appreciate the apology for your brother, but there's nothing you need to do to make up for him. Have a good day, and I hope you're driving home."

I stepped back, then turned around and walked to my car. I heard sneakers on the pavement, keeping a respectful distance but still following me. I reached the driver's side door and turned to find him standing on the other side of the car.

"Take me with you."

My eyebrows shot up in complete surprise. "I'm sorry, do what?"

"Jay's miserable and I'm uncomfortable and they're his friends, not mine. And I'd like to talk to you some more."

"It's Christmas Day. Where am I supposed to be taking you?"

"Anywhere. Waffle House. The parking lot at the mall. Let's just..." He turned, glanced at the house, then turned back and winked at me. That pretty brown eye *winked at me.* "Jay will probably pass out soon, and then I'll come back and take him home. Let's escape for a while."

4

I slid into the car, closing myself in when I shut the door behind me. I could just back out of the driveway, away from these people ruining my holiday even more than it would normally have been.

I thought he was crazy. Stone cold nuts. But... intrigued, I pressed the button to unlock the door. He smiled and pulled the handle, then slipped inside next to me. The interior of the car filled with the scent of his cologne—cool, crisp, woodsy with an edge.

"So..." I eyed him.

"So." He stared at me.

"Where am I supposed to be taking you? Everything's closed."

He shrugged a shoulder. "Doesn't matter. Just... away from here."

I sighed and put the car in reverse, then backed out of the driveway and meandered through the subdivision until I got to the main road. There were a few shops, restaurants and bars along the highway. I prayed something close would be open.

Minutes later, after wandering streets that resembled more

ghost town than booming metropolis, I pulled into the parking lot of an Italian restaurant that was open and bustling with business.

"We can at least get dessert, some coffee. Sit awhile."

"This works for me," said Will, already stepping out of the car and heading to the front door. He held it open, and I walked inside, where I was enveloped by the scent of fresh garlic bread and marinara sauce.

"Two please," I told the hostess, who showed us to a table in a sunny corner of the restaurant. I flipped right to the end and perused the dessert menu, trying not to feel odd about being on an impromptu date with a man I didn't know, who was the brother of a man I used to date, who had summarily rejected me not once or twice but three times in the span of a few hours.

"Why don't we get the dessert platter?" He suggested. "It comes with options and we can both try a few things. I don't know about you, but I can put away some sweets."

"Sure, if you want." I closed my menu and slid it to the edge of the table. "So. You and Jay aren't full brothers. How much younger are you?"

"Four years, almost. We have different mothers."

"You must both take after your father."

Will smiled. If he could blush, he'd probably be the shade of a Red Delicious apple. "Is it that obvious?"

"Like looking at a set of twins, practically. But you seem much different from Jay."

He folded his arms and settled them on the table, shrugging a shoulder. "Not saying I can't be a jerk now and then. I'm human. But nah, I don't drink like him."

"How long has he been like that? And is that why his wife left?"

"He doesn't handle stress well. The business nearly failing almost did him in. I'd say it's been building for a while but only got really bad in the last year."

He sipped a few swallows of the water the waitress had left. "And yes. That was a big reason his wife took off. The drinking, plus not having any money... she said that wasn't what she signed up for. I guess I see both sides."

"Both sides?"

"Yeah. I get her point, but I also believe that marriage vows are real. In sickness and in health. For richer or for poorer and all that."

"But if he's calling her names, getting drunk, not taking care of her... she's supposed to honor some vows? That's far beyond rich or poor, sick or healthy. What about his vows? His role?"

I shook my head, taking a few swallows of water myself. No sense in getting worked up about a man that dumped me to date several women of varying race and size. I had no dog in this fight.

Will chuckled and leaned forward. "Let's not talk about my brother. He's taken up too much time and attention that I want to spend on getting to know you."

My face burned hot. I couldn't look at him for very long, otherwise my thoughts would trend toward pathways it hadn't traveled in a long time. It had been... *a while*... since I'd had more than brotherly thoughts about a man, since I'd craved powerful arms around me and the scent of masculine cologne and the deep tenor of a voice that made me feel like I was safe.

"Alright. Let's talk about something else."

"Okay." He smiled, his eyes twinkling at me. "You must not have family close by if you spend Christmas with Faith and Anthony."

It was an innocent enough observation, at least I was sure he thought it was. But the question had, for years, made me uncomfortable. It forced a conversation that I hadn't been getting better at enduring. And though I knew I didn't have to have the conversation, I wanted to.

"Uhm. No, not really. My parents..." I blinked, attempting to keep my emotions at bay. "I have some aunts and uncles scattered around, but Faith and Anthony are my only close family."

A shadow crossed his face. His gaze dipped to his water glass, then flicked back up to me. "I'm sorry. I was curious. I didn't mean to bring up a sore subject."

"It's okay. I don't talk about them often. Not everyone needs to know my business."

"You can talk to me. I'd love to know more about you. Everything about you, actually."

I almost laughed and had to stop myself from rolling my eyes. "Is that so? You're curious about your brother's college ex-girlfriend?"

"Sure. I'm curious about all kinds of interesting things like... what kinds of books you like to read? What does your name mean? What's your signature drink? Do you travel? What do you think about when you're alone, in your quiet time?"

I laughed. "You're pretty damn curious. So, I like to read a little of everything. Biographies, self-help. Some crime drama, a little romance, some literary highbrow. And yeah, I like to read children's books to the babies at the nursery."

"Okay," he said, laughing. "We have some interests in common, though I have a heavy daily newspaper and Time, Newsweek, Financial Times habit." He sipped more water and waved a hand at me. "Go on."

"Uhmm..."

I shifted in my seat, unbuttoning my light jacket and slipping it from my arms to lay it on the seat next to me. Not only was it warm in the restaurant, Will's pointed, steady gaze with those dark eyes was heating my insides to a near boil. I could hardly breathe under his stare.

"My name is Arabic; It means 'fortunate'. I like a glass of cabernet, but I'd rather an Amaretto Sour if you know what you're doing. I love to travel. Faith and I take a trip every year when I'm done with my school year. I usually need it," I finished with a sigh and a roll of my eyes.

He nodded. "You're a teacher, right? Yeah, I understand that. You deserve it." Will paused, though still staring. "And?" He prodded.

"And... what?"

"The last question. What do you think about in the quiet times, when you're alone?"

I was grateful the waitress stopped by to take our orders. I added coffee to our dessert platter and by the time she left our table, I still wasn't sure I could even get the words out.

"I really never talk about this. And I'm not sure why I'm talking about it now. But..."

I pulled my phone from my purse, unlocked it, and opened it to the photos app. There were several that I never deleted, that I looked at every day.

"When I'm alone, in the quiet time, I think about my parents." I flipped to a photo and turned the phone around so Will could see it. It had been taken in Jamaica at my parent's thirtieth wedding anniversary. The beautiful, chocolate brown couple bore wide smiles and had their arms around each other. "Five years ago today, there was an accident. I'd picked them up from the airport after this trip. They were excited, telling me all about their vacation. I was driving, it was raining, I got distracted. I would have seen the drunk driver cross over the median if I'd been paying attention."

I flipped to the next photo, one of a man who had proposed to me only weeks before. "My fiancé and my parents were in the car. My parents were killed. He suffered severe injuries, but he survived." Will's mouth made a perfect 'O' shape as he stared at the photo. "But he broke off our engagement a few weeks after he got out of the hospital."

I clicked the button along the side of the device, locking it and sealing the photos away again. Sealing away my past again. "The driver who hit us totaled his car, but walked away from the accident with minor injuries. He's serving ten years for vehicular homicide. He'll probably be out in a few years. Then he can resume his life, I suppose."

I frowned. "My parents will still be dead. My ex-fiancé will still walk with a limp."

"I am so sorry, Saidah. I... I really am. I didn't mean to bring up a painful memory."

"It's not so much painful as... *there*. Always there. It's been five years and I still associate this season with losing my parents. With losing a man I thought loved me enough to honor those vows he was about to take. With knowing that even though that driver was *sorry*, being sorry and eating three squares and watching The People's Court every day doesn't make up for the past five years."

"Of course not. Nothing makes up for losing your parents, losing someone you love."

I glanced up and offered him a wry smile, blinking back tears. "Wow. I really went there. I'm maudlin on Christmas. I need some new memories, I guess."

Will reached across the table and took both of my hands into his. His fingers, coarse with the markings of manual labor, rubbed the backs of mine. Every swipe of his fingers across my skin was soothing.

"Maybe you could associate today with being invited out to a glass of wine or an author lecture or... somewhere down the line, a little getaway somewhere. I'm sure Faith is a great travel partner, but I know my way around an all-inclusive resort."

My eyes narrowed and my head tilted to the side. I was confused. I'd heard his words, but... "Are... you trying to suggest that we date?"

An eyebrow rose. "Any reason we can't? Or shouldn't?"

"Well, I used to date your brother."

"I'm not concerned about that at all. Jay's definitely not concerned."

"And you're four years younger than I am–"

"Three and a half, if you're the same age as Jay. And I'm definitely not concerned about that. We get along, so far at least. I'm old enough to know what I need to know. I'm mature and responsible. Besides, my grandmother used to say, 'a new broom sweeps well'. You know what that means?"

"No. What?"

"It means younger men do it better."

That made me laugh. Loudly. I hadn't really laughed in so long that it made my throat hurt.

"So, what about you, then? You and Jay don't have any family here? Is that why you're freeloading at Faith's dinner table?"

"Sort of. Jay and I have two sisters, also half sisters. Papa was a rolling stone, I guess. Did you know that?"

I shook my head. As much time as I spent with Jay, we weren't good for... talking. And the more time I spent with Will, the more I saw what my life would be like, had I ended up with Jay. And I was so grateful that he'd been a little playboy and dumped me.

"So, you know, mom and dad are gone. We have some family, but they're spread out. We usually run a tight work schedule, so traveling for the holidays is tough. I normally spend Christmas with Jay and his wife, but this year..." Will rolled his eyes and laughed.

"You don't have someone special that you share holidays and once-yearly occasions with?"

"Well, I guess I should come clean," he said, after a moment of hesitation. The way my heart threatened to gallop out of my chest was frightening. If this man was about to show me his girlfriend, I was going to go *off*.

He pulled out his phone and scrolled a few photos. He handed the phone to me, a smile trying hard to twist his lips out of the smirk he was giving me. "That brat right there has me wrapped around her fingers. Or her paws."

I looked down at the phone and smiled at the miniature puff of fluffy white fur that seemed to pose for her glamor shot. "Aww," I cooed. "What's her name?"

"Coco. She's a Bichon Frise, about three years old. Spoiled as hell. Other than her, I don't have anyone I share my special moments with." He smiled wide, then. "I'm working on it, though. Got someone in mind."

Our dessert arrived and then the coffee arrived. We bickered softly over who would get to try the double dark chocolate cake first; who would get the last bite of cheesecake; which of us would take the tiramisu home.

I asked Will a litany of questions, from where he attended high school to his college major to his preference for tea over coffee and nonfiction over fiction. And, for the first time in five years, I was smiling. Laughing. Enjoying myself. And not feeling guilty about it.

In my bag, my phone vibrated. I waited until Will was sliding his credit card into the leather envelope to check it.

Faith Thomas: *Girl. WYD??!!*

I giggled as I tapped out a message in response. *On our way back soon.*

Faith Thomas: *That is not even what I asked you. Where are you? Why did ya'll leave this drunk fool here for us to deal with?*

We needed to escape. So we left. Had some dessert. Talked. Really talked. He's cute!

Faith Thomas: *I spent hours making two cakes, and you two left CHRISTMAS DINNER to go eat dessert somewhere?*

Did I mention he's cute? When is the last time I said somebody was cute? And he is nice, unlike his brother. He was trying to make up for Jay. How is he, by the way?

Faith Thomas: *Passed out and drooling on my suede couch!*

After he bitched about his wife for an hour. I told Anthony to never invite anybody over here ever again.

I'm sorry, but I'm cracking TF up. We're on our way back. Will will take his brother home and he'll be out of your hair.

Faith Thomas: *And then I am going to put these kids to bed and drink an entire bottle of wine.*

Faith Thomas: *And don't think you're getting out of telling me about this whirlwind date you decided to go on.*

I laughed. locking the phone and tucking it back into my purse. Will stood, then reached for my jacket, holding it while I slid my arms into it.

"Ready?" He asked. I nodded, slipping my hand into his. "We in trouble?"

"Oh yeah," I answered, snickering. "It was worth it, though."

"It really was," he said, grinning over at me. And then that brown eye winked at me again.

5

I WAS in no hurry to get back, so I took my time, meandering through the neighborhood, the bare tree branches kissed by the rose glow of dusk. Talking to Will had become easier, the more time we spent together. I suddenly had so much to say and someone new to say those things to. I only hoped he felt the same.

I pulled into the driveway behind the SUV. I chuckled, again, at the parking job. "Did Jay drive here?"

Will dipped his head, an embarrassed half-grin on his lips. "He picked me up. I shouldn't have let him drive."

"I hope you don't have too many problems getting him out of here."

"Me too. And he and I are going to have a talk about his drinking. He could have hurt someone." Will glanced over at me, not with pity but a gentle sympathy.

I smiled back, grateful that he'd internalized what it meant to me to lose my parents the way I did. "It would mean a lot to me if you'd talk to him about that. Tell him about my parents. He can make up for today by not hurting anyone else with his drinking."

"Sure." He sighed, his gaze traveling to the front door of the house, a brilliant red against the light toned brick. "I guess I'd better get in there and rescue Faith and Anthony, but... could I..."

"What?" I asked when he paused.

"I can't decide what to ask first—to kiss you or to see you again."

I let a sultry chuckle fall from my lips. "The answer is going to be yes, either way."

"Just in case I didn't make it clear... I apologize for my brother. Deeply. But from now on, things are going to be about me and you. I'm going to call you tomorrow and we're going to talk about things that have nothing to do with Jay Hunter. How does that sound?"

"Deal," I started to say, but it was cut off by warm, thick lips dusted with sugar from multiple desserts. I moaned, twisting in my seat to get closer, but he pulled back and broke off the kiss. To say I was disappointed would be an understatement.

"Gotta leave you something to look forward to." He winked at me. That gorgeous eye *winked at me again*. The dome light popped on as he opened his door and exited the car. "Goodnight, Saidah. Talk to you tomorrow. We'll do some more work on reshaping your Christmas memories."

"Okay," I said as I exhaled a breath. I'm not even sure I said the word. "Goodnight, Will."

The front door opened, spilling light from indoors into the yard as I pulled away. I should have gone inside, talked to Faith, gossiped about my date, had some wine and some more cake...

But I wanted to be alone. And not in a bad way. I wanted some time to myself, to sit and remember and smile about my afternoon, to think about something besides the images that had plagued me for years, the sadness and the loss that had been my constant companion, but now seemed to have ebbed away.

I had a new Christmas memory and a small spot of hope. I wanted to spend some time thinking about that, for a change.

"I'm so looking forward to a few days off," Faith mused, weaving between the aisles at HomeGoods, one of her favorite stores. Sure, there was Williams Sonoma, Kitchen Virtue or the Food Network shops, but Faith found the best gems on the racks and shelves at HomeGoods. "The kitchen closes tomorrow and we don't open up again until New Year's Eve."

"I hear you."

She glanced over her shoulder to cut her eyes at me. "Mkay, says she who has been off work for a week already. I knew I should have been a teacher. You get all kinds of vacation."

"I *need* all kinds of vacation. Those kids are two full-time jobs. Add the 'at risk' qualifier and I don't even know why you're complaining about me getting time off. I don't want to see those beautiful brown faces until January 3rd at the earliest."

"I guess," she said, sighing. "Then can I be jealous about your post-Christmas plans, at least? I mean..." She reached for a ceramic tea-kettle and tipped it up to peer at the price tag. She grimaced and set it back down. "Jamaica? Isn't Will laying it on a little thick?"

"You know what this is? Payback. You've been married,

what... thirteen years now? Do you know how many stories I've had to listen to about your happily ever after? Dozens. *Dozens*, I say. You just settle down over there, old married lady, and listen to *my* happy stories."

"Well, not-so-quietly, I'm excited that you have happy stories. Especially this time of year. It's so nice to see you smiling, and out and about, your place all decorated again. Tell your stories, girl. Don't let the fact that Anthony has never surprised me with a trip to Jamaica over the holidays deter you from bragging your face off, ok?"

"How come you don't sound committed to that statement?"

"Cause I'm *not*. I'm salty as hell. Tell Will to tell Anthony the honeymoon ain't over in the Thomas household. He can still woo me. I can still be impressed."

Faith waved a hand over the hodgepodge collection of cookware and utensils and frowned. "There's nothing here I can't live without. Let's go get some hot chocolate and a cookie. You can help me finalize Christmas dinner."

Faith and I left the store and headed to her small SUV parked a few spots from the door. As we climbed into the vehicle, I uttered a quiet admission. "I'm a little nervous about this trip to Jamaica. I mean, I told him I wanted to go, because it was the last trip my parents took before..."

I swallowed the lump trying to form in my throat. Nearly six years and I still couldn't talk about my parents. I was working through it, though. I'd finally started seeing a therapist to take my life back from the tragic accident that took them from this world.

"It's not the same resort, is it?"

"No, no. Not the same resort." I shook my head. "But it's still... I don't know. Is it creepy to want to go there? To repeat the last vacation they took, to want to see the spot where they sat and took that last picture?"

"Not... *creepy*, no. But do you think you'll find something there? Some kind of meaning or closure? You'll probably be disappointed, if you're expecting a big emotional moment."

"I don't know what I think, Faith. I just know that I feel like I need to go."

"Then you should go. And if someone thinks that's creepy, well..." She shrugged a shoulder, then pressed the ignition button. The vehicle rumbled to life. "They don't have to live your life, do they?"

No, I mused. I supposed they didn't. And, as of late, my life had been pretty damned good, and I wanted to live it myself.

I'd met Will on Christmas Day the year before, at Faith's house. Her husband had invited my old college flame to dinner and, despite my plans to sack out on the couch watching Christmas movies and drinking spiked cocoa, Faith lured me to her house.

Where I took the leap towards healing and let someone climb over that fortified brick wall I had built around my heart.

"Please promise me you and Will will not disappear halfway through dinner this year."

I snorted before I took a sip of my salted caramel latte. "I make no promises. Especially since you let your husband invite Jay again."

Faith sighed loudly and rolled her eyes before dropping them to the notepad sitting in front of her. She had listed what she planned to cook for Christmas dinner and was trying to cobble a shopping list out of the menu.

"I told Anthony that if we have a repeat of last year, that I will send him and Jay somewhere by themselves. Hell if I let him ruin dinner two years in a row, not when I'm making my prime rib with horseradish cream. The only reason he is coming this year is to apologize for last year."

"Yeah, well, I've had my share of spending time with him. His AA journey has been inspiring, and I'm happy he and his wife have reconciled, but he's still the same insufferable buffoon from college. I don't even know what I saw in him."

"So it's still not weird, dating your college love's younger brother?"

"He's not my college love. He's a guy I dated. And no, it's not weird. Will is nothing like Jay. That's what I love about him."

I grinned, knowing I was beaming from my wide forehead to the tips of my toes. But it was okay. I was crazy in love and it felt good.

"Speaking of Will," I noted, checking my watch. "He's probably in the kitchen. It's his night to make dinner and I like to help."

Faith nodded, tipping back the red paper cup to sip the last of her hot chocolate. "I'd better head home, too. Anthony has had the girls all day. I can only hope he hasn't burnt the house down trying to make pizza."

"He'd better not. I want my prime rib with horseradish cream."

7

———

"Honey! I'm home!"

I unlocked the door and swept inside the condo, dropping my purse on the table in the entryway and pulling my jacket from my shoulders. It had rained; I made it home in time to save my fresh Dominican blowout.

I heard a sharp bark, then saw a streak of white careening around the corner, paws sliding on the wood floors, she was in such a hurry.

"Hi, punkin!" I reached down to pick up Coco, laughing at her body wriggling in my arms and the soft sandpaper scrub of her tongue against my cheek. "You're exactly who I hoped would come running when I said *honey, I'm home*. Where's Will? Huh, girl?"

"Kitchen!" He called, though I could have figured that. Will loved to cook and savored the nights when it was his turn. Between him and Faith, I had worked in an extra Zumba workout, because hell if I was ever missing a meal.

At the mention of his name, he poked his head around the corner and smiled. "I'm elbow deep up a chicken's ass or I'd run down the hall and lick your face, too."

"Just one thing licking my face is enough. Let me wash up and take off my shoes and I'll be right in."

"Take your time," he said, heading back to the kitchen.

I hung a right into the bedroom, dumping Coco on the bed, where she curled up in her usual spot on Will's pillow. We had been dating about six months when we decided to go for it and move him and Coco to my place. Will didn't want to renew his apartment lease, and I owned a place, so although it seemed early, things had worked out perfectly. They fit right in, like they'd always been there, and I hardly remembered what life was like before Will. And Coco.

I slipped into the bathroom to wash my face, take off my jewelry and pull my hair behind a thick headband, then changed out of my comfortable jeans and blouse into even more comfortable leggings and a long Albany State t-shirt. I left the bedroom and headed down the hall where I could either go to the kitchen or to the living room.

I chose the living room, just to look at the tree. I adjusted the stockings hanging from the fireplace — there was even one for the dog. My eyes floated over the collection of holiday cards we'd received from friends and family, including Faith and Anthony, and Jay and Celeste, who were making a tenuous effort at reconciliation.

My heart warmed at the festive trinkets that Will and I had picked out together, and the sprinkles of holiday cheer that I hadn't thought twice about setting out, filling out the space.

Behind me, ice clinked into a glass and I heard the familiar sounds of Will mixing a drink. I reached behind the tree to flip the switch to turn on the lights — the small pearl bulbs on the tree, the multi-colored lights around the windows in the living room and the two beaded angels at either end of the fireplace. Those were my parents, watching over me.

"How was Faith?" Will asked, handing me a glass. I took it,

sipping a little of the Amaretto Sour that he had perfected to my taste.

"Ready for vacation so she can hang out in her own kitchen. And she's mad at you."

"Me?" Will dropped onto the couch, lifting his feet up onto the ottoman, as was his habit. He set his drink on a coaster on the table in front of him and patted the cushion next to him. I did, curling my body into him. "Why's Faith mad at me?"

"Because you haven't talked Anthony into taking her to an island for the holidays. So she's mad at you."

Will laughed. I enjoyed hearing the sound through his chest and my ears. "I don't have anything to do with the Thomas household. Anthony's gotta work that out for himself. Did y'all talk about the menu for Christmas?"

"Mmmhmm. She's making her famous prime rib—"

"With the horseradish cream," he said, wistful. I practically heard him lick his lips.

"Yep, her tradition. Plus the usual sides — potatoes, something green, homemade rolls. And that macaroni and cheese you liked last year. She said to tell you she's using smoked gouda this year."

"I'm already hungry for Christmas dinner. But I liked something else better than the macaroni and cheese." He closed his arms around me, making sure that a hand traveled a wide swath across my thigh to my backside.

"You flirt," I told him, giggling.

"Only for you. You're a little older than me, you know. You might go find an old man to be with."

"Three and a half years is nothing. Besides, I've been with an old man. Your grandmother is right. A new broom does sweep well. So well."

"I feel like that's a dig against my brother. And since we're still deep into sibling rivalry, I'll consider that a win. We just won't tell him."

"That wouldn't be awkward at all." I gulped down a swallow from my glass before setting it on a coaster. "But he'd need to unpack that in therapy. And then wax on about it at every opportunity."

"He's making excellent progress, though. Let's not make too much fun."

"You're right. I'm in therapy, too, so I shouldn't joke about it. But I don't put everyone through the experience of me going to therapy."

"Mmm." He hummed, his lips brushing against my temple. I knew he wanted to ask how it was going, how I was feeling. We had agreed that I didn't have to talk about it, but from time to time I shared small things with him.

I'd told him about the night my mother came to me in a dream. It was relatively soon after I'd met Will and things were going well — so well it scared me. We had a good, long mother-daughter talk.

Will said if I thought my mother came to me, she must have. I wanted to think — it gave me comfort to believe it, but my therapist helped me understand that it was more likely that my mind was telling me it was time to move ahead. Maybe I was waiting on a sign that said I could smile again. It was okay to be happy.

That I was *still here*. That I could live my life.

"I was going to help you with dinner. I thought you were elbow deep up a chicken's ass?"

Will laughed into the air, his head cocked back. "You like that line. Prep didn't take long at all. I just put my dry rub on the chicken. Had to get it all up on the inside, too. Then I set it on a can of beer and put it in the oven. I thought we'd have some artichokes—"

"Wait." I blinked, confused. "You did what with a beer?"

He smirked, his brows knit together. "You've never had beer can chicken? We had it all the time, growing up. Dad made it on the grill, but I've perfected it for the oven. I had a taste for it. Had to buy a can of beer specifically to make it. You'll like it."

"There's not much I don't like, in the way of food, if you're making it. Actually…" I stretched to press my lips to his in a warm kiss. "There's not much I don't like if it has anything to do with you."

"The feeling is very, very mutual, baby."

Coco trotted down the hall and leapt up onto the couch, into Will's lap. She loved me, but she *loved* Will and she was a jealous little dog. She made her way into the room if she heard the slightest hint of a kiss.

"Including your dog."

"I told you she was a brat." He lifted her and set her on the couch, then tapped my hip. "You can help me with the vegetables, though. We need to chop and slice."

"I think we can call Beer Can Chicken a hit."

Will's eyes dropped to my plate, which held a leg and thigh bone that had been picked clean, remnants of steamed artichokes with hollandaise sauce and scant evidence that I'd been served a generous helping of roasted broccoli-cauliflower mix.

"You think? Did you leave anything on the bone, babe?"

"Nope. And I ate all of my vegetables."

"That you did. I'm proud that I make vegetables that you'll eat."

Will got up, reaching for my plate. I playfully smacked his hand. "I'll get the dishes. You know what this is — you cook, I clean."

"But you helped cook…"

"I chopped broccoli and cauliflower, Will. Hardly any effort at all. You did the heavy lifting. Sit."

I grabbed his plate and mine, shoveling what we left of our dinner plates into the garbage compactor, then placed the plates and silverware in the dishwasher. Will was a neat cook. He washed as he went, put away spices and utensils after he used them. I didn't mind cleaning up after him when he hardly made a mess at all.

The nights I cooked... well, I tried. Will didn't complain when he had to clean up after me.

In a few minutes, I had put away the leftovers, put the rest of the dishes in the dishwasher, wiped down the counters and stove and swept the floor. The dishwasher hummed quietly.

Will was in the living room, where he lounged with his feet up on the ottoman, flipping through the recent issue of The Financial Times. Coco perched in his lap like a queen on her throne.

"Someone's comfortable," I commented, scratching her behind the ear. "I think I'm going to run myself a bubble bath and relax, read a little."

"You sure? I can—"

"I'm sure. Faith dragged me to nine stores today. *Nine*. I'm a little sore. Maybe later on we can uhmmm... stretch." I gave Will a wink, then laughed because he was the one always winking at me.

"I can definitely stretch some things for you." Will grinned, his tongue swiping his bottom lip as he gave my backside a tap. "Go. Enjoy your bath. I'll meet you in bed."

I must have been tired. One minute I was sinking into a piping hot, bubbly, jasmine scented bath and resting my neck on a rolled-up terrycloth towel. The last thing I remembered thinking was how peaceful and happy I'd been lately. Unbelievably happy. But instead of being afraid that it was going to be taken from me, I was excited. I sensed... something. Something on the horizon. I remembered sinking into the tub, my mind on those happy, expectant thoughts.

The next moment, Will was bent over me, shaking me awake.

"You're gonna get all pruny and wrinkly. And not that I wouldn't still love you, but I don't want you to get all pruny and wrinkly."

I sat up, yawning and stretching my limbs. Then smiled as I watched Will pull the plug in the tub and grab a fresh bath sheet from a stack in the linen closet. He opened it and stepped back, waiting for me to get out of the tub, then wrapped it around me.

"Come on, sleepy. Let's see if we can get in some stretches before you fall asleep on me."

"That nap might be just what I needed, you know." I laid across the bed on my stomach. Will and I had a funny little ritual where he liked to apply my body butter after a bath. "I don't feel all that sleepy right now."

"Is that right?" I felt Will's weight on the bed, and then his lips skittering across my skin. Goosebumps rose in waves.

8

I CLUNG TO WILL, my arms wrapped tightly around him, my legs locked around his torso. The steady thumps of the bed against the wall and the matching rhythmic sound of skin against skin was heady and erotic. I wanted — *needed* to climax, but I also never wanted him to stop.

His body writhed with long, hard strokes until I couldn't take it anymore. My back arched as I convulsed and I let out a peal of loud, pleasured moans. A few moments later, his voice chorused with mine.

I panted into the air, trying to catch my breath. Will had collapsed on top of me, still inside me, his mouth laying little suction kisses on whatever skin he could get to. When he attempted to pull out and roll away, I gripped him with my legs so he couldn't move.

"Are you trying to tell me something?"

"Yeah. Don't move. I might be in the mood for some more in a minute."

He chuckled. "You're gonna wear me out. Or is that the point?"

"Nah," I answered, then finished with a snort. "Just taking advantage of this new broom situation."

"My pleasure, then."

Deciding that he wasn't going to move soon, he settled his body weight onto mine and bent his head to kiss me. "I love you, Saidah. Way more than I ever thought I could love a person."

An eyebrow lifted. "More than Coco, even?"

"More than Coco, even. I'm sure she's real upset about that, too."

As if on cue, I heard a light *scratch-scratch* at the door and the whine of a spoiled Bichon Frise on the other side of the bedroom door. If we didn't lock her out, sex was... interesting.

"I love you too, Will," I murmured softly, stretching up to kiss him. "Even if I have to compete with the dog."

He moaned through another kiss, then rested his forehead against mine. Pensive, he opened his mouth, then closed it.

"What?" I prodded.

"I uh... I wanted to talk to you about something. I've been kind of... well, waiting until I felt like the time was right."

"Oh?" I unlocked my legs and sat up. This sounded serious, not a conversation one should have while intimately joined. Will sat up, then flipped the comforter back, the warmth of the room making short work of the sweat glistening on his body.

"Let me... I'll be right back."

He hopped out of bed and headed for the bathroom, coming back moments later to slip into his side of the bed. I sat up on my side, rod straight. Something about the serious tone he'd used put me on edge.

"Don't let me down easy. Just say whatever it is."

"Babe... relax. It's not anything bad. We're okay."

The sigh of relief that I let out was so loud, it made him laugh. Then he felt bad about laughing, so he rolled his lips inward and tried to bring his face to a neutral expression.

"I uh... I mean, we've talked, for the past few months, about things we wanted to accomplish, either on our own or together. It's been a great year, hasn't it?"

I nodded in agreement. The year *had* been great. I had taken on a new role at the school. Outside of the children I usually worked with, I now had a small, dedicated group of students for one-on-one study and guidance. It meant more work, but I found it rewarding to see them grow with just a little of attention. And over the summer, I had been placed in charge of coordinating volunteers at the Children's Nursery. I still read to them, but now I could encourage others to do the same.

"The business has grown so much in the last year," Will was saying. "That Panola Road project put us on the map. I've become a much better salesman. We've got projects going nonstop. We've had to hire a few people, subcontract some others. And I moved in with a beautiful woman that I fell in love with."

He smiled, glancing at me like I could miss that bit of sucking up. "I feel like I'm in a place where... well, I'm happy. But I'm looking forward to more. I want more, and I want more with you. I guess I wanted to get a pulse check. See how you're feeling about things. About us, about... life."

I almost laughed aloud.

Life was like night and day since I'd met him, almost a year to the day ago.

He'd called the next day, just like he promised he would. He took me to a Speakeasy. It happened to be a spoken word night, so we listened to authors and poets read their work for the small but lively crowd. We had drinks and talked. And then went for coffee and dessert and talked. And when I'd called him to let him know I got home safely, we ended up talking most of the night.

When I thought I was all talked out, that this man couldn't possibly find anything interesting about this broken woman he'd met on Christmas Day... he'd call and we'd talk more. About everything. About nothing. About important things. About stupid things.

Before I knew it, a few months had gone by and I was falling in love. And terrified of it. The fear was irrational, and I knew it, but I couldn't help it. I'd lost people I'd loved. I didn't think I could take it, if something happened and I lost him, too.

I almost pushed him away. *Almost.* Instead, I picked up a phone and made an appointment.

Therapy was rough at first, the hardest thing I've ever had to do. Baring my soul, exposing my vulnerabilities felt impossible. That wall I'd built around myself, around my heart? I was so afraid to tear it down. And I had so much guilt to work through — about the accident, about living after my parents were gone.

After I got used to talking to Dr. Sawyer, it got easier. It wasn't like I was cured or healed overnight, but I didn't cut things off with Will. The thing I was most afraid of — losing him — didn't happen. Our relationship got better.

And *better.*

I knew what he was asking, though. Was I still scared?

Did I still want to take things impossibly slow, so I didn't get hurt?

Was I far enough along in my progress to see past the next few days, the next few weeks, the next few months with him?

And the big question... was I ready to risk my heart again? To commit to taking vows, seriously. For better or worse? Richer or poorer?

I reached out for him, placing my hands on his chest, pushing until he was on his back, shoulders pressed against the mattress. Then I hiked a leg over him and straddled his waist.

"I think... life is pretty damned amazing, thanks in some part to you. My life is completely different from it had been for a long time. I'm grateful to be where I am. Where we are. I'm right where I want to be, Will. If it's okay with you, I want to stay here forever."

His hands roved my body, around the curve of each generous cheek before moving to the junction of my thighs. The tip of a finger dipped into my core, collecting wetness before circling and stroking, stirring me up again.

"That's fine with me," he mumbled, his eyes flicking up to mine. I bent to capture his lips in a slow, sensuous kiss while his fingers worked their magic. "That's... just fine with me."

9

———————

"Ready for this?"

Will put the car in park and glanced over at me. He smiled, except his smile was devilish and made me laugh. He knew I was nervous and already had one foot out of the door. I was ready to bolt if Jay was the slightest bit disagreeable.

"I guess. Do we need to set up a signal? So if something happens and we have to leave, you'll know?"

"How about you just say *let's go* and we'll walk out."

I sucked my teeth, then gathered the straps of my purse. "Smart ass. He's not ruining two holidays in a row."

"He didn't ruin last year, though," said Will, leaning over the armrest to nip my ear. "Not for me. And not completely for you. Right?"

"Right. But you know what I mean—"

"Yes, I know what you mean. I've got your back. I'm not afraid to knock a sucka out for disrespecting my woman, even if he is my brother." He reached for the door latch, saying, "Let's go in. We're already late."

"Whose fault is that?"

"Well, it wasn't *my* idea to spend the whole morning in bed."

"Oh. Yeah. I guess that is my fault."

I leaned over to kiss him, my lips lingering on a moment longer than usual. I had wanted this year to begin the exact opposite of how last year began. No sadness, no melancholy, no dearth of holiday joy and gratefulness for all that had come to me throughout the year. And I wanted to take advantage of having someone with me to ring in the season. Mission accomplished.

I got out, then waited for Will to grab the wine and gifts from the back seat and meet me in front of the car. Then I tucked my arm into his and we walked up the driveway and the front walk.

The bright red door swung open as soon as we reached the landing. Anthony stood in the opening, Avery perched on his hip in a pretty, bright red dress and white stockings.

"Merry Christmas," he called out, offering his free hand to Will to shake, then wrapped the same arm around my shoulder as I passed him into the house. "If this dinner sucks," he muttered in my ear, "we're all running away."

I laughed, giving little Avery's leg a tug as I followed Will inside. As was customary, Faith had transformed the house into a Winter Wonderland. The tree was just as grand as it had been the year before, except this year the motif was a soft dusty rose, a deep midnight blue and silver accents.

Will bent to slide a few boxes under the tree, then took the wine over to the bar and set it inside the silver bowl full of ice. He turned, pulling down the hem of his new cashmere sweater, just in time to come face to face with his brother, Jay.

They worked together, but I hadn't been in the same room with Jay more than a few times since last year. My pride was still hurt. I still smarted from the things he'd said to me. I was a believer that alcohol didn't invent thoughts and feelings; rather, it removed the filter that kept them at bay in polite company. We were fully grown mature adults, older and wiser, but he'd resorted to childish name calling and insults.

He had never apologized. I decided not to hold my breath, waiting for it.

"Hey, man," Will said in greeting. They shook hands, then gave each other manly slaps on the back. "Looking good. Where's the Mrs.?"

"In the kitchen, with Faith. Getting pointers on how to make prime rib or something. Like she cooks."

Jay turned to me, and his eyes lit up. He and Will were so close in resemblance that they could be twins, but while he was a handsome, tall, muscular specimen of a man, my heart didn't skip beats and my hands weren't clammy and I wasn't nervous when I saw him.

It's amazing what being in love can show you.

"Saidah," he said, his greeting to me the warmest it had ever been. He leaned over to drop a dry kiss on my cheek. "You look beautiful. My brother is a very lucky man." He thumbed over at Will, who beamed a knowing smile in my direction.

You would know, I thought. Out loud, I said, "Thank you, Jay. Merry Christmas."

"Thanks. You too." He clapped his hands together, then rubbed his palms against one another. "Well. Here we are again. It's... a little strange to be here again. After last year..."

"Let's let last year be last year. And let's move away from the bar," Will suggested.

"I'm okay," he insisted, but his gaze had already settled on the bottles. Will wrapped an arm around his shoulder and walked him away.

I exhaled a long, loud breath and left Will and Jay to themselves, headed for the kitchen.

Faith and Jay's wife were deep in conversation over the prime rib, sitting beautifully on a serving platter. "I just mix a few ingredients; less is more, you know."

"Do you just make it up? Or do you use a recipe?"

"Truth be told," Faith said in hushed tones, "I use Alton Brown's Horseradish cream recipe. It's great and I don't feel the need to improve on it."

Celeste nodded, her perfectly arched brows angled closely together in conversation. I'd first met Celeste — thin, tall, model-gorgeous, lightly toasted cinnamon skin tone Celeste — at Faith and Anthony's wedding. If the daggers she had shot in my direction throughout the wedding and reception were any sign, she knew about our brief relationship and wasn't pleased to even be sharing the same air with me.

These days, I could tell she tried not to let it bother her — I was with her brother-in-law and visibly happy, but depending on how the reconciliation was going, some days and some encounters were better than others. I prayed tonight's dinner would be one of the better ones. Faith deserved to not have two ruined Christmases.

And I had absolutely no desire to take her man. She could keep that rude son of a —

"It smells so good in here," I commented, bending to sniff a deep whiff of Grade A beef, roasted to perfection. I knew Faith had put her foot in this meal and I was looking forward to enjoying it.

"Oh," said Celeste, her birdlike mouth painted in bright red lipstick pursed in a tense bow. She backed up a step or two and folded her thin arms across her chest. *"You're* here."

Thinking about Jay's subtle dig at her a few moments ago and her reaction to me, I gathered that things weren't going well between them.

"I'm here," I confirmed, giving her the brightest smile I could muster. "Merry Christmas! Will brought in gifts for you and Jay. They're under the tree."

Celeste didn't respond, save an eye roll she thought I didn't see.

"Saidah!" Faith's face lit up and her arms closed around my shoulders in a tight hug, like we never saw each other. "Thank God you're here," she mumbled in my ear. "Please don't leave me alone with these miserable people."

I almost laughed aloud, but caught it before my giggle could spill over. I guess I'd made a reputation for myself as a person who would leave a room if I wasn't satisfied.

"I'm here for the duration," I assured her, then stepped back, surveying the room. Food covered every surface. Delicious smelling, great looking food. "Tell me what to do. Put me to work. I'm ready to eat."

"Okay, grab a dish and set it out on the buffet. Saidah, you know how I like it — main dish in the middle veggies on the right, carbs on the left."

I grabbed a dish and walked past Celeste to arrange dinner on the buffet. When I walked back into the kitchen, she was still standing there, her arms still crossed.

"Chop chop, Princess. We all work around here. Grab a dish so we can eat."

Celeste huffed, flipped her blonde weave behind her shoulder and reached for the smallest dish she could find.

I wanted to laugh. Out loud. Uproariously. Jay Hunter got exactly who he deserved.

On my way out of the room, I gave in and let out a loud chuckle.

"What's funny, baby?" Will asked.

"I'll tell you later," I whispered, dropping an obviously loud smooch on his lips, then heading back to the kitchen.

I passed Jay, grinning like a fool. And betting he was watching me walk away.

During dinner, Will, Anthony and Jay were wrapped up in a sports conversation, something about which quarterback on which team they'd switch out for Colin Kaepernick. Faith, Celeste and I chatted about after-Christmas sales and *Real Housewives of Atlanta* while Faith tried to monitor the girls in their booster seats and Christmas dresses.

I tried not to have a drink, since I felt it was rude to pour up while Jay was still going through his steps. He'd stopped drinking on New Year's Day and had been diligently working to repair his life, including his marriage. The jury was still out on that, but I didn't want to do anything to harm his progress.

But Jay insisted that everyone enjoy themselves, so I sipped on a glass of wine while I took a break from stuffing myself silly.

Honestly, I couldn't wait until Will and I could get home, get comfortable and have a drink together. I grinned to myself at the thought of *home*; my cozy little condo that I shared with the man I loved. And his dog.

"Saidah," Anthony called from his end of the table. "It's great that you made it to our table two years in a row. Maybe it'll be a new tradition?"

I shrugged, coyly brushing off the question. Will and I had had that brief conversation a few nights ago, but a question hadn't been asked. I had no doubt that it would be, but until it was, I couldn't speak for my future Christmases.

Next to me, Will dropped his arm from the back of my chair to rub my shoulder. "Or," he replied, "maybe we'll have our own traditions."

"My bad, man." Anthony sat back in his seat and pushed his nearly empty plate away, then reached for the glass of bourbon he'd been drinking. "I didn't know things were serious like that."

"Yeah," Will nodded, his eyes meeting mine. "Things are serious like that." The sparkle in those brown eyes was so...

impish. He had something up his sleeve. Before I could ask what was up, he scooted his chair back from the table and stood.

"I had planned this for later, but... serendipity, I guess. If we could just all.... I don't know, take a break from dinner and uhm... Saidah..."

He reached for me, his hand outstretched for mine. "Join me at the tree?"

Chairs scratched the wood floors as everyone pushed back from the table and migrated from the dining room to the living room, where they spread out among the couches and chairs. Will and I stood in front of the beautifully lit Christmas tree.

Will grabbed my hand and held it in his. I noticed that his palm was clammy, and he was trembling. I gave him a squeeze and tried to catch his eye as he pulled me close.

"So, like I said, I'd planned for this later. Maybe after dessert, when everyone's full and comfortable. But Anthony had to open his big mouth about traditions and... well..."

He chuckled, giving the room a nervous half smile. "If you don't mind, before you plan for Saidah to be at your table every year, I thought I'd ask if she'd mind being at mine."

He paused, turning to face me, then gripped both of my hands in his. My heartbeat sped up, wildly thumping. I was sure the room could hear it pounding out of my chest. Everything seemed to happen at lightning speed, but in slow motion at the same time. Like I couldn't keep up, but I wanted to rush past this moment to The Big Moment.

"You know how you just... know things? Like you always knew you wanted to be a teacher. You never had to wait to decide you wanted to teach; you just knew. That's the same way I knew, when I met you, that you were the one for me. That's the same way I knew I was in love with you. And it's the same way I know that... uhmmm..."

He released my hands and sank to one knee, pulling a small

velvet box from his pocket. When he popped the lid up, I almost couldn't see the ring nestled inside for the tears in my eyes. My head whipped around to Faith, who was trying — and failing — to keep a straight face. It was impossible that she didn't know about Will's plans, considering the cushion ruby halo engagement ring was exactly something I'd fawn over, then lament that I didn't have someone to present one to me.

And she'd tell me to keep the faith, hang in there, there's someone out there, just for me. I used to think that was just something she said, an automatic response. Then I met Will.

"As I was saying, it's the same way I know that I want to spend the rest of my life with you. So, I think I know the answer, but I'm nervous, anyway. I'm still asking, though. Saidah Harlan, would you do me the honor of being my wife?"

I nodded, my head bobbing viciously, since I was crying so hard I couldn't speak. Will pulled the ring from the box and slipped it onto my finger. It fit snug and it was gorgeous, sparkling in the lights and against my skin. I grabbed his forearms and pulled until he was standing, then fell into his arms.

"I love you," he said, his lips so close to my ear I felt his breath on my skin. "I wish your parents could have been here, but I have a feeling they're watching over you, and they're happy."

"Yeah," I answered, sighing happily, my arms still tight around his shoulders. "I think they are. They would love you, Will. Absolutely love you, just like I do."

And just like that, my Christmases for the next... forever were locked in.

"THANKS FOR HAVING US," I told Faith while she helped me pull on my coat. It was chillier this year than last year, which I loved because we could turn on the fireplace and sit together — with Coco between us — and watch a movie. I was looking forward to doing that exact thing as soon as we got home. "Those leftovers will not last long. Will is primed for a midnight sandwich."

"He might not be hungry again by midnight, the way he ate today. I love a man that appreciates good food."

"Me too. Especially that one."

I looked back at Will, who was giving Anthony a hearty hand-shake with one hand, balancing the containers of leftovers with the other. He was guarding them like military secrets.

My gaze returned to Faith. Her expression softened as she smiled. "Enjoy it, Saidah. He loves you more than anything, and you deserve all of that love. Let him show it. All the way through that vacation in Jamaica."

"I knew you couldn't hold back your saltiness." I smirked, then plopped a kiss on her cheek. "Thanks for your help. I know you were a huge part in orchestrating today."

She nodded. "It was the only reason I would let Jay back in

my house. I'm happy for you, honey. You deserve a happily ever after. And besides," she said, leaning in so only I could hear her. "How awesome is it that Jay had to watch you get engaged to his brother while he sits next to a woman that only came back to him because his business turned around?"

Her eyebrows did a little dance when she pulled back. Then we burst into laughter.

"That's the most awesome part. I'll let you know we made it to Jamaica; our flight tomorrow is crazy early."

"You don't worry about me at all. Just let that man spoil you and enjoy yourself. I hope you find what you need there."

"We ready?" Will asked, coming up beside me. "Coco is probably doing the potty dance."

I slipped my hand into Will's and nodded. "Pretty sure I already found what I need."

"Thank you for today."

"Oh, no baby. Thank *you* for today. I've never been so nervous in my life."

We'd come home and changed clothes and were comfortably perched on the couch with the dog and some spiked hot chocolate and a few slices of Faith's pound cake. The fireplace was lit and so was the tree and all the lights and the angels, too. My condo was so festive, it was ridiculous.

"There was no need to be nervous. I knew just like you did. I just needed a little time, was all."

"What a difference a year makes, right? I only came to dinner to make sure my brother didn't drive into a tree."

"And I only came to dinner because Faith tricked me."

"And all it took was me and you being in the same room."

"Do you believe in fate? Or destiny?"

"Hmmm." Will mused, then dipped his head to brush his lips across mine. "I didn't used to. I'm a logical person. But I think I have to, now."

"Me too, baby. Me too."

"I know I put you on the spot, in front of your friends, my family. You're welcome to back out, you know."

I lifted my left hand, gazing at my ring and how it sparkled so brightly in the lights from the tree. "You'll pry this ring from my cold, dead hands, Will Hunter. I love you, I'm marrying you, I'm having your babies and we will be happy for the rest of our lives. Got it?"

"Got it," he said, laughing. "And this trip to Jamaica... are you going to be okay?"

"Yeah. I'll be great. In fact, I was thinking..."

I twisted in his arms so I could face him and grabbed one of his hands. "Let's treat this as a... a prelude to a honeymoon. A celebration. I don't want to think about their last vacation or see where they took their last photo. I'm done with all of that sadness, with keeping things inside because I feel guilty about being happy, being so stupid in love. I want to celebrate us in the same place *they* celebrated. That's it."

Will nodded slowly, letting me know he'd been thinking the same thing.

"My brother is still an asshole, even when he's sober." I groaned. AA was helping, but I still couldn't believe I ever fell for him. "But if it wasn't for him, we would have never met. And I never would have had the chance to be this happy."

I picked up our glasses and handed Will's to him, then clinked mine against his in a toast.

"Here's to finding unexpected love and happiness."

Praise for DL White

It's been a minute since a book kept me up all night reading but I could not let this one go.

— REVIEWER

Well-written, great story line...highly recommend.

— REVIEWER

Well worth the time spent, engaging story line with a couple of interesting twists.

— REVIEWER

DL White has done it: written a wonderful book about friendship and all its foibles in such a way that you don't want the book to end.

— KIM, KIM TALKS BOOKS

Acknowledgements

Some may recognize parts of this book from a short posted on my website around 2015. The story niggled at me, because it didn't really have a conclusion. I was supposed to be working on a different project but I couldn't get Saidah and Will out of my mind, so I finally pulled it down and started filling out the story. It's still a short! But it's a happy holiday story that I hope you'll love.

Many thanks to my Betas for being willing to read through the drafts and seeing the diamond in the rough (if y'all only knew what a mess my stories were before the Betas get a hold of them!) to make this short shine the best it can for the readers. You are much appreciated and I cannot do this without you!

Thanks also to my fellow author #frans, especially my Atlanta writer's group, who help me to be a better Writing Ass Writer.

Also by DL White

Thank you for reading this novel and I hope you enjoyed it! If you're interested in other books I've written, you can the list below:

Pick up my titles in eBook, print or audio at Booksbydlwhite.com/books

Brunch at Ruby's, a Ruby's novel

Dinner at Sam's, a Ruby's novel

Beach Thing, a Black Diamond Romance

Elysium, a Black Diamond Vacation Romance

Leslie's Curl & Dye, a Potter Lake Small Town Romance

Second Time Around, a Potter Lake holiday short

The Guy Next Door, a Potter Lake Small Town Romance

The Kwanzaa Brunch, a holiday short

A Thin Line

The Never List

Hey, Lover